'06
14.95

A Note to Parents and Teachers

Kids can imagine, kids can laugh and kids can learn to read with this exciting new series of first readers. Each book in the Kids Can Read series has been especially written, illustrated and designed for beginning readers. Funny, easy-to-read stories, appealing characters and engaging illustrations make for books that kids will want to read over and over again.

To make selecting a book easy for kids, parents and teachers, the Kids Can Read series offers three levels based on different reading abilities:

Level 1: Kids Can Start to Read

Short stories, simple sentences, easy vocabulary, lots of repetition and visual clues for kids just beginning to read.

Level 2: Kids Can Read with Help

Longer stories, varied sentences, increased vocabulary, some repetition and visual clues for kids who have some reading skills, but may need a little help.

Level 3: Kids Can Read Alone

Longer, more complex stories and sentences, more challenging vocabulary, language play, minimal repetition and visual clues for kids who are reading by themselves.

With the Kids Can Read series, kids can enter a new and exciting world of reading!

Pup and Hound
Lost and Found

For Hollie, my family's puppy love — S.H.

For the Roske "pups" — L.H.

Kids Can Read ® Kids Can Read is a registered trademark of Kids Can Press Ltd.

Text © 2006 Susan Hood
Illustrations © 2006 Linda Hendry

Kids Can Press acknowledges the financial support of the Government of Ontario, through the Ontario Media Development Corporation's Ontario Book Initiative; the Ontario Arts Council; the Canada Council for the Arts; and the Government of Canada, through the BPIDP, for our publishing activity.

Published in Canada by
Kids Can Press Ltd.
29 Birch Avenue
Toronto, ON M4V 1E2

Published in the U.S. by
Kids Can Press Ltd.
2250 Military Road
Tonawanda, NY 14150

www.kidscanpress.com

The artwork in this book was rendered in pencil crayon on a sienna colored pastel paper.
The text is set in Bookman.

Series editor: Tara Walker
Edited by Yvette Ghione
Printed and bound in China

The hardcover edition of this book is smyth sewn casebound.

CM 06 0 9 8 7 6 5 4 3 2 1
CM PA 06 0 9 8 7 6 5 4 3 2 1

Library and Archives Canada Cataloguing in Publication

Hood, Susan
        Pup and hound lost and found / written by Susan Hood ; illustrated by Linda Hendry.

(Kids Can read)
ISBN-13: 978-1-55337-806-8 (bound) ISBN-10: 1-55337-806-7 (bound)
ISBN-13: 978-1-55337-807-5 (pbk.) ISBN-10: 1-55337-807-5 (pbk.)

I. Hendry, Linda II. Title. III. Series: Kids Can read (Toronto, Ont.)

PZ7.H758Pupl 2006   j813'.54   C2005-903893-4

Kids Can Press is a *corus*™ Entertainment company

Pup and Hound
Lost and Found

Written by Susan Hood

Illustrated by Linda Hendry

Kids Can Press

What was that —

that *vroom, vroom* sound?

Look, Pup!

The truck is going to town!

So Pup and Hound

leaped from their chair.

6

They hitched a ride …

... to the county fair!
Flags and banners flapped
in the sky.
"Yip, yap!" barked Pup
as a blimp flew by.

Hound sniffed the air.

He sniffed something dandy —

hot dogs and pretzels

and — oooh! — cotton candy!

Pushing their way
through people's knees,
Hound hurried Pup
past a circus of fleas.

They stopped for a snack.

They begged for a treat.

A little girl gave them

all they could eat.

The loudspeaker blared,
"Friends, take your places!
It's time to begin
the Poky Pig Races!"

Ten squealing piglets raced
around the track.
But Pup wandered off
when Hound turned his back.

Hound watched the piglets

race on and on.

When he turned around —

oh, dear! — Pup was gone!

"Woof!" There he was

behind the hay bale!

No, it was just a pony's tail.

Wait! Over there!

Were those Pup's paws?

No! It was a cat

with very sharp claws!

Was that little Pup?

Look! Right up there!

No, it was just a teddy bear.

Hound sniffed the ground.

Where would Pup go?

Would the man on stilts

or the juggler know?

Hound tracked Pup's trail

from place to place.

He dodged little kids

in a three-legged race.

He looked in each barn.

He looked in each stall.

He asked all the cows.

No Pup at all!

Hound looked high.

And Hound looked low.

Where was that Pup?

Where did he go?

Wait! What was that?

Hound heard people clapping!

He picked up Pup's scent,

then heard his friend yapping.

Hound raced past the barns,

past some sheep and a goose ...

31

... to find Pup in charge
of the kissing booth!